The Seals Who Flew Home

About The Marine Mammal Center

The Marine Mammal Center in Sausalito, California is the world's largest marine mammal hospital and rescues more animals than any other organization in the world. The Center covers a rescue range that spans 600 miles of California coastline plus areas in Hawai'i.

Sick and injured animals receive the highest quality of care at the Center's state-of-the-art veterinary facilities, which can care for up to 300 seals, sea lions, and other marine mammals at one time.

About the Author

In addition to this book, Patricia Arrigoni, one of the co-founders of The Marine Mammal Center in Sausalito, California, is the author of four editions of *Making the Most of Marin*, a guidebook, as well as *Harpo the Baby Harp Seal.* a children's book. She also developed the script for *Silent Predators*, a television movie for the Turner Broadcasting Network, and she has produced a fifty-six-minute DVD entitled *Old-Fashioned Fun on Route 66*.

The author has been syndicated with Garnettt News Service, Copley News Service and Creators Syndicate. She has published over 500 features in newspapers and magazines.

Publications by This Author

Books

Making the Most of Marin: A California Guide

The Marine Mammal Center: How It All Began: Recollections of One of the Founders

Harpo the Baby Harp Seal

Whistles, Smoke, and Steam

Video

Old-Fashioned Fun on Route 66: A Story of the Road Travelling Between Two Eras

Major Motion Picture

Silent Predators

(produced by the Turner Network)

Sergio and Sabrina greet residents of The Marine
Mammal Center in Sausalito, California.

The Seals Who Flew Home

Patricia A. Arrigoni

Co-Founder, The Marine Mammal Center
Sausalito, California

Illustrations by
Anastasia Simonenko

Travel Publishers International
Fairfax, California

Published by Travel Publishers International Corporation
www.travelpublishers.com

Library of Congress Control Number: 978-0-962546-85-3

Printed in the United States of America

Design andproduction: Janet Bollow Associates
Illustrations and cover art: Anastasia Simonenko

Distribution managed by Janet Bollow Associates
For all inquiries contact: janetbollowassociates@gmail.com or (415) 717-2291

Contents

CHAPTER ONE
A Terrifying Illness Sweeps the World   3

CHAPTER TWO
Secret Marine Mammal Council Meeting   9

CHAPTER THREE
A Long Bicycle Ride   13

CHAPTER FOUR
Getting into The Marine Mammal Center   19

CHAPTER FIVE
A Talking Harbor Seal Issues a Warning   21

CHAPTER SIX
Family Struggles with Deadly Pandemic   29

CHAPTER SEVEN
Sergio Searches for Military Drones   33

CHAPTER EIGHT
Kids Caught Taking Pictures of Hidden Drone   39

CHAPTER NINE
Sergio and Sabrina Study Neptune Drone XXL10   45

CHAPTER TEN
Plans Are Made to Push Drone Idea   47

CHAPTER ELEVEN
Kids Are Featured in Drone News Stories   53

CHAPTER TWLEVE
Operation "DRONE HOME!"   57

CHAPTER THIRTEEN
Commander Hires Drone Operator   61

CHAPTER FOURTEEN
Sea Lions Fly to San Francisco Bay   67

CHAPTER FIFTEEN
Kids Photos Appar in Sunday Newspaper   75

CHAPTER SIXTEEN
Plans for More Seal Releases   77

CHAPTER SEVENTEEN
Neptune Flies Marine Mammals Home   81

CHAPTER EIGHTEEN
Sergio Plots a Dangerous Flight   83

CHAPTER NINETEEN
Sergio Stows Away   87

CHAPTER TWENTY
Seals and Sergio Are Pitched into the Ocean   91

CHAPTER TWENTY-ONE
Sabrina Sees Sergio Fall   97

CHAPTER TWENTY-TWO
Sergio's Survival   101

CHAPTER TWENTY-THREE
A Desperate Call to Sabrina   105

CHAPTER TWENTY-FOUR
Near Disaster for the Drone   109

CHAPTER TWENTY-FIVE
Alice Reunites with Her Family   113

Toby, a young elephant seal, is rescued by four young
volunteers from The Marine Mammal Center.

CHAPTER ONE

A Terrifying Illness Sweeps the World

A worldwide pandemic was sweeping the world, and nearly every public business had shut down. People were getting sick, lots of them. Some people were even dying. They were catching a disease from each other that was like a bad cold or flu but much worse. Also like the flu, it could easily spread from person to person.

It was a virus, known as COVID-19, and life in countries around the world changed almost overnight. It was called a "pandemic," which means the illness was spreading everywhere.

The world famous Marine Mammal Center in northern California, located on hills above the Golden Gate Bridge, had released hundreds of volunteers. Because of the virus, all the young scientists in training there had left to return to their homes throughout the United States and Europe. The employees who stayed wore facemasks and other protective gear. They tried to be as careful as possible by washing their hands all the time and staying at least six feet from each other. It meant this special hospital, just for sick seals, sea lions, and other marine mammals, was operating with a small crew. Luckily, most of the rescued animals were healthy now. Many had been released back to their ocean homes before everything was shut down.

But a few seals were still waiting for their release. Among themselves they had formed what they called the "Marine Mammal Council." None of the human staff still on duty was in on their secret. Emergency meetings of the "Marine Mammal Council" were held secretly at night. Although there was a human night crew in these perilous times, most of the workers had left the pools area, except for feeding, so the seals could talk freely among themselves.

About a dozen members of the Council included four California sea lions, three Pacific harbor seals, two northern fur seals, two sea otters, and one young northern elephant seal.

For years when a day for release arrived, marine mammal patients had been hauled back to sea in heavy carrier cages that were lugged across sand by humans. Eventually, large rubber wheels had been added to the carriers, which was a big improvement, and now flying drones could lift the carriers right out to sea, an even more massive improvement. How wonderful, they all felt.

So, now stuck at the Center, the seals were plotting an escape back to their homes. They planned to secretly commandeer the military drone carrier. They knew it was stored in the old NIKE Missile site that was underground not far from their pools. It could fly them most anywhere in the world. Somehow they knew that NIKE missiles had been used by the United States Army as an anti-aircraft missile system to protect the coastline of California. They had heard that "NIKE" is a Greek word for "Victory." One of these missiles was stored at Fort Cronkhite. They were certain that was a big important deal.

These days a human could set a series of dials, push a few buttons, and the drone would rise like a helicopter to fly away to whatever beach was scheduled for the release. If everything went according to their plans, the Harbor seals would be flown to the Bolinas Lagoon, just a short way north of San Francisco.

The California sea lions wanted to head back to San Francisco Bay, to a place they knew about called Pier 39. Sea lions had been hauling out on the docks there for a long time. Maybe they would meet up with their family and friends!

Toby, a young northern elephant seal, decided to go home to the Point Reyes National Seashore, not too far from The Marine Mammal Center.

When was it that he had arrived at The Marine Mammal Center? That day seemed so long ago. Toby remembered that he had been out swimming along the shore with his mom that day when heavy clouds had moved in, and it had gotten very windy. Soon the ocean around Toby and his mom had been churning, and the waves had become the biggest Toby had ever seen.

Toby remembered that his mom had bellowed over the wind, "Toby, stay close to me." He was naturally a good swimmer, but he was young, and the waves had been too much for him. When the storm at last calmed, Toby had barked out for mom, but she was gone. He was alone.

Toby remembered, being scared and tired and swimming towards shore, but when he finally got there, he was so exhausted, all he could do was rest on the sand. He had cried out for his mom, but she couldn't hear him, so Toby had slept alone on the beach that night.

When he woke up the next morning, Toby really had started to worry. He had been lonely and so hungry. His mom had always been there when he needed food, but not now.

Soon Toby noticed something happening on the beach–humans! Uh oh! Mom always had said to be careful around humans. He didn't know then that these humans were from the nearby seal hospital, The Marine Mammal Center. On that day, he didn't even know there was a seal hospital. They were there because someone had called them to report a seal pup alone on the beach.

These humans seemed different. Toby had been pretty sure that these people would help him. They had handled Toby so gently and carefully. They spoke to Toby and told him that everything would be all right now. Soon he was feeling a little better.

Then, the people had put Toby in a big metal carrier, loaded him on one of the rescue vehicles from the Center, and headed down to Sausalito and the hospital.

When they arrived at the Center, expert doctors and scientists had taken over, just like at a human hospital. The doctors had gently checked Toby all over. Then several of the volunteer staff had transported Toby to a special pen where there was a little pool of salty water just for him. But best of all, he had a big breakfast of herring – his favorite. Back then he was just big enough to chew and swallow smaller fish. If only his mom had been there. Toby was safe but lonely.

Returning to the problem of where the marine mammals would be released, the "Council" said it was clear that the sea otters only had to be flown south to the kelp beds off the coast of Monterey.

The Northern fur seals would probably be returned to San Miguel Island, one of the Channel Islands off the coast of Santa Barbara in Southern California. They had been rescued all tangled up in fishing nets.

Finally the "Council" argued about whether or not they needed human help for this break out. They all knew that they would be returned home eventually, but the pandemic might go on for a long time and they wanted to go home NOW!

Alice, the harbor seal in the pool, meets with
members of the Marine Mammal Council. Front:
Hugo, a juvenile sea lion; Six-pack, another
harbor seal; and Toby, a young elephant seal.

CHAPTER TWO

Secret Marine Mammal Council Meeting

Young Toby, the elephant seal, was still growing. When older, his nose will have grown a lot. Now, he flopped his 500 pounds of belly blubber around on the cement by the pool so he could face Hugo, a 600-pound sea lion.

Hugo had been brought to the rescue center with a gunshot wound in his large chest. He probably had been shot by a fisherman who did not want sea lions competing with all the fishermen for food. It had taken a four-hour surgery to remove the bullet, but the sea lion had recovered and was ready to go home. Only the pandemic was holding things up.

"We do need help with the drone," Toby remarked scratching his nose with an enormous flipper. Hugo twitched his ears, stretched his neck, and puffed out his chest with a sigh. "How about that tall, lanky kid who comes up on his bike all the time?"

"Is he a volunteer here?" Toby asked.

"No," another Council member answered, "he's too young, only maybe twelve or thirteen. He's usually wearing jeans and an old faded sweatshirt, red, I think. He has a younger sister who follows him around a lot too, probably eight or nine years old. She wears jeans, too, and a pink and white sweatshirt, and she has a long ponytail."

Alice, one of the harbor seals swimming in a nearby pool stopped to listen. "I know who you mean," she said. She put her flippers on the side of the pool and pulled up her fat little body. Anyone looking on would have noticed the brown spots on her nearly white body. "I think those kids live down in Sausalito. They are out of school now because of the pandemic. I've heard that their grandmother has been helping them with some online studies because their schools are closed."

Hugo looked at Alice with interest. "How do you know all that?"

Alice rolled over to let the sun dry the pool water on her tummy. "I heard them talking the other day. Their mother is a flight attendant, and their father is a doctor. He's been very busy with the COVID outbreak."

Toby looked interested. "They might be able to help us," he mused. "What else do you know about them?"

But Alice had decided to dive back into the pool for another swim. They all waited.

"Do you know their names?" Toby asked while blowing air out through his big elephant seal trunk-like nose. It sounded a little like drums.

Alice swam over to the steps of her pool and hauled herself up. "I think she called him 'Sergio,' and he called her 'Sabrina,' and the last name sounded something like 'Sulla.' The boy wants to study marine biology someday."

"That sounds really encouraging," Hugo, the sea lion observed. "Have you ever tried to talk to them?"

Alice hesitated. In the marine mammal world it was strictly forbidden to converse with humans.

"Well, maybe just a few words," she replied.

"What?" Toby asked.

"I just said 'Hello,' and Sabrina said 'Hello' and 'What is your name?' and I told her. That was all."

"Perfect then!" Toby exclaimed. "You will be our speaker."

For the rest of the night the Marine Mammal Council discussed how they might persuade Sabrina and Sergio Sulla to set up the drone for their big escape.

Sabrina and Sergio ride bicycles through Sausalito,
California on their way to The Marine Mammal
Center. San Francisco Bay is in the background.

CHAPTER THREE

A Long Bicycle Ride

At their home in Sausalito the next day, Sergio and Sabrina Sulla finished their online lessons, ate some lunch, and headed outside. They stopped to grab a face mask on the way out. Both just slid the masks over their head and let them hang around their necks. It would be difficult to pedal a bicycle and breathe through the cotton mask at the same time.

It was a beautiful spring day in Northern California with wildflowers, especially orange poppies, appearing everywhere. The view from their house showed slightly choppy water in the yacht harbor, and beyond several large sailboats were skimming the water of San Francisco Bay. The air smelled fresh with just a light breeze.

"I'm going up to The Marine Mammal Center," Sergio declared zipping up his sweatshirt.

"Can I come?" Sabrina asked anxiously as she zipped up her own. She hoped her big brother was in a good mood today. There was nothing else to do because all her friends were studying at home.

"Oh, I guess," Sergio replied. Sometimes his little sister drove him crazy, always tagging along. "All the guys are still busy with school work until 2:00 pm. You and I just start our classes earlier."

"But they are all locked down now," Sabrina said while pulling her bike out of the garage. "Where is Mom today, anyway?"

"I think she flew to Hawaii. She had to work the early morning flight," replied Sergio while pulling on his bicycle helmet.

"How can we get into the Center if it is all locked up?" Sabrina asked adjusting her helmet over her long ponytail. She really wanted to go with her brother.

"I know the lock combination. One of the volunteers let me in last year after hours." Sergio explained.

The two took off riding down the hill from their house into downtown Sausalito and south through town along Bridgeway Street. They passed the park at Plaza Vina Del Mar and all the tourist shops and seafood restaurants along the waterfront before heading up toward the freeway.

Traffic was light with most of the businesses closed. Even the usual mob of bicycle riders from San Francisco was absent today.

Arriving at the turnoff that led to the five-minute tunnel, they took a right and lined up behind a couple of cars waiting for the light to change. This old single-lane tunnel was built by the military long ago and connected Fort Baker to Fort Cronkhite where The Marine Mammal Center was located.

After a few minutes, several cars came out of the tunnel headed for San Francisco or somewhere in Marin County, and then the kids could cycle through. Fortunately, a few years ago the military had restored the tunnel, so it was not as dark and creepy.

It took them about ten minutes to ride through the now well-lit tunnel and into a big park named "The Golden Gate National Recreation Area." They rode past the old military barracks that are now rented to park employees and then jolted over several speed bumps in the road.

Beyond the barracks the hills were green and wildflowers bloomed. A stiff breeze ruffled their clothes. Both kids could smell the grass and the ocean in the distance.

"Head for Rodeo Lagoon," Sergio yelled pointing to some directional signs. A breeze blew straight into his face.

"I know," Sabrina answered. A wind was blowing her ponytail straight out behind her.

When they reached the lagoon, both pulled over to catch their breath and look out over the wooden bridge that connected the park road to the sandy beach. They both had attended many sea lion releases at this beach. Now it, too, was closed and empty because of "shelter-in-place" rules that had been started to prevent the spread of the coronavirus.

After a few minutes the kids headed their bikes up the last hill to The Marine Mammal Center. Past the empty parking lot, they reached the locked gate.

Sergio climbed off his bicycle and studied the lock. Then he quickly punched in some numbers, and the gate opened. "Let's leave our bikes out here," he suggested. "We can hide them in that tall grass over there and hike the rest of the way up."

"Sounds good," Sabrina replied as she climbed off and wheeled her bicycle to the side of the road. Then her dark eyes sparkled as she added, "I made kind of a friend the last time I was here." Silently she hoped her big brother would not start teasing her.

"What are you talking about?" Sergio asked as he attached his helmet to his bicycle handlebar.

"One of the harbor seals, probably from the Bolinas Lagoon at Stinson Beach, a female named 'Alice' said 'Hello.' So, I said, 'Hello' back."

Sergio looked at his younger sister in astonishment. She was a bit shorter than he, about 4 foot 5 inches, while he had shot up the last year to be almost 5 foot 8 inches. But he thought she was still such a silly kid, thinking she talked to a harbor seal. She always did have a huge imagination. He remembered all the little dollhouses and the schoolhouse she had once set up with her imaginary pupils. Sometimes he had overheard her talking to the neighborhood dogs that she included in a backyard tea party. That had lasted for several years. No point in getting into an argument, though, as there was no one else to hang out with these days.

"O.K." he replied sarcastically. "Take me up and introduce me to Alice, the talking harbor seal." They climbed up the final hill to the Center.

Did You Know?

Did you know that seals and sea lions are also called pinnipeds?

Sabrina and Sergio disinfect their boots before
entering the pens at The Marine Mammal Center

CHAPTER FOUR

Getting into
The Marine Mammal Center

The Marine Mammal Center, rebuilt from an old military site in 1975, was perched on the top on a hill that had sweeping views of Rodeo Lagoon and the Pacific Ocean beyond. There was usually fog in the morning, but by now it had burned off, and the water was glittering in the warm sunshine.

The pools were located in the back, sheltered by structures that held solar panels on their roofs. Marine mammals were divided into separate pools depending on their species and the nature of their sickness or injuries.

Under normal conditions around 1300 volunteers would be busy working in shifts around the clock taking care of all the animals. Today there was was only a small crew on duty and most were in the kitchen preparing formulas of fish and medicines to feed the current patients.

Alice, who by now was quite a fat little harbor seal, saw them coming. She swam frantically around her pool, barking a warning to other members of the Marine Mammal Council in nearby pools. Immediately everyone was on alert.

On the hill above, young Toby, the elephant seal, heaved himself up on the edge of his gigantic pool. It was so large it could even be used for a young whale if necessary. He had quite a ways to come down for the Council meetings, which were always held in the dead of night. Now he hoped he could hear everything. So much depended on this moment.

Sabrina talks with Alice, the harbor seal
and Sergio is very skeptical.

CHAPTER FIVE

A Talking Harbor Seal Issues a Warning

Sabrina splashed ahead in her big boots. "The harbor seals are toward the back," she told Sergio. "And don't make a lot of noise. No one is supposed to know they can talk to us."

Sergio walked behind her and rolled his eyes. "Yeah. Sure." What a drag, he thought again, that he always had to take his little sister with him.

They arrived at the pool for harbor seals. Alice was already out of the water and waiting for them. "Hello Sabrina," she said.

Sergio leaned forward and let out a cry of shock. 'WHOA!" he bellowed looking back and forth between his sister and the harbor seal. "WHAT IS THIS? SOME KIND OF JOKE?" This couldn't possibly be happening, he thought.

A young woman came out of the kitchen and called to them. "Hey Sergio, everything all right down there? Hi Sabrina." Caroline McGowan, age twenty, had started as a volunteer at the Center and was later hired to help feed the marine mammals. She was above average height, 5 foot 10 inches, with blond hair worn long. Her blue eyes appeared soft and warm in a welcoming way, making her quite a beautiful young woman.

She loved The Marine Mammal Center so much that she used to commute from Oakland all the way across the San Francisco Bay to volunteer. She even had a permanently damaged finger where a baby elephant seal had bitten into a joint. The wound had gotten infected and never healed properly.

Still, she always had a big smile. At this time she was studying marine science at the University of California in Berkeley, but with classes suspended, these days she worked online.

"Hi Caroline," Sabrina said. "My brother just tripped but he's OK." Sabrina hoped that Sergio would quit yelling. Sometimes he was an absolute embarrassment.

Caroline called back. "We are going to be bringing out some buckets of fish in a little while if you want to watch the feeding."

"Cool!" Sabrina called back. "That would be so much fun!"

Caroline returned to the kitchen, and Alice watched her intently until she was sure she was completely inside.

Sabrina turned back to the harbor seal. "This is my brother, Sergio." She held her breath hoping her brother wouldn't start yelling again.

"Hello to you, Sergio," Alice said. She shook her body, and water sprayed on the kids. They brushed it off laughing.

The pools next to Alice's pool were suspiciously quiet as all the animals strained to hear the conversation that was about to take place. Even Toby and Hugo were silent for a change.

Sergio stood speechless staring at the harbor seal. Finally he stammered, "You… you… you can really talk to us? Why now?"

"We need help!" she said. "Since the pandemic started, most of the volunteers have gone home, and we have had almost no releases here even though most of us are healthy now. We want to go home!

"Besides," Alice went on, "we need to warn our families in all the places that we live about the dangerous virus. It now looks like a virus can be passed from humans to us. I have been told that some people think it might have come from an animal market in China and was passed to humans. Now if the opposite can happen, it could wipe out whole colonies of seals!"

"The most common virus in marine mammals, especially monk seals, is *morbillivirus*," she continued, "which is passed by breathing. The Center has been testing us for viruses using swabs, and some of us get vaccinated. Our families need to know to head for the water when any human appears. If we don't warn them, they could all die!" Large harbor seal tears rolled down Alice's cheeks, and she wiped them away with a front flipper.

"There's nothing Sabrina and I can do about that," Sergio said. He pushed back a lock of hair from his forehead as he stomped around in his rubber boots. "You will just have to wait until the lockdown is over."

Alice heaved a large sigh. "That could be a long time. First, a vaccine has to be invented. I know some formulas are being tested now, and then if something is found that actually works, it will have to be mass-produced. Then all humans need to be vaccinated, and that could take years. I miss my family! We all do," she declared extending a flipper around to the other pools.

"I guess we could unlock some gates for you," Sabrina suggested.

Alice shook her head. "We already learned how to do that! We just need you to operate the drone."

"DRONE! WHAT DRONE?" shouted Sergio. He appeared clearly suspicious.

"SHhhhhhhh!" replied Alice with a flipper pointed toward the kitchen door. "The big drone that is stored in the NIKE silo. It showed up last month."

"Where did it come from?" Sergio asked. He seemed to have forgotten already that he was talking to a harbor seal. His face was strained as he concentrated on what she was telling him.

"A U.S. Coast Guard Commander had it brought to the Center. It is large enough to carry two or three of us," Alice explained.

"What does it look like?" Sabrina asked.

Well, it's not as big as a regular plane. I was watching when they drove it in on that uncovered truck carrier. It has big blades like a helicopter to take off straight up into the sky and ski-like pontoons so it can land on water. I think it is supposed to be top secret. I believe it was designed to drop Navy Seals into the water. Apparently, this one had some defect."

The kitchen door opened and Caroline came out carrying a bucket of small fish. She had a mask covering her nose and mouth. Sergio and Sabrina immediately pulled up their masks, which had been dangling around their necks.

"Feeding time!" Caroline yelled as she pulled on a pair of rubber boots and cleaned them by sloshing around in the tubs of disinfectant near the pools.

Alice quickly dove back into her pool, and then barking started from all the other marine mammals.

Sergio and Sabrina were silent as they watched Caroline enter Hugo's pen. Caroline's assistant, Noah, held up a flat board with a handle on the back that kept Hugo from lunging out of the gate when it opened. All the marine mammals seemed to want to escape the pen every time they were fed, especially the healthy ones.

Sabrina watched intently as Caroline and Noah skillfully maneuvered their way into the pool area and secured the gate behind them. Then she laughed as she watched Caroline toss each fish into the air over Hugo's pool and saw him lunge for the food. But it bothered her that each animal seemed to want out so badly. She had always thought of The Marine Mammal Center as the most wonderful place on earth where marine mammals who were orphaned, sickened from toxoplasma, caught up in fishing nets, or even shot, as Hugo had been, were rescued, nursed back to health, and then released back to their home territories. But these weren't normal times. She would have to ask her mother how long she thought COVID-19 was going to last.

Caroline arrived in Alice's pen and Sergio and Sabrina were delighted to see that the harbor seal was also expert at catching fish tossed to her mid-air.

When Caroline had finished feeding Alice, her bucket was empty and she returned to the kitchen for more fish.

Sabrina whispered to Sergio. " We need to think about all this."

He nodded in agreement. Maybe his little sister wasn't so crazy after all. He had really learned a lot today, and it seemed weird that he had actually had a conversation with a harbor seal. And the military drone! That was really exciting!

Alice's head popped up from the water, and Sabrina spoke quietly to her. "We need to consider this."

Alice nodded and dove back into the water for another swim and to check out the pool for any fish she might have missed.

It was shortly after the children left that Alice had a visitor. It was "Six-Pack," another harbor seal from the Bolinas Lagoon who had been rescued when he became tangled up in the plastic rings that hold a six-pack of soda cans. His pool was being cleaned, so he was temporarily staying with Alice.

Six-Pack and Alice greeted each other and then Six-Pack said somewhat timidly, "I heard you talking about the drone. Is that really true that they are thinking of flying us home in it? Aren't you. . . well . . . maybe a little scared to go up in that thing?"

Six-Pack waved a flipper to get Alice's attention. "I saw it arrive and thought that maybe it wouldn't be such a great idea for anyone to fly in a plane without a pilot."

"It's not supposed to have a pilot," Alice replied, "and honestly, I was thinking myself that it might be risky, and, yes, it could be dangerous. But I so miss our little island home in the lagoon. I get tired of swimming endless circles in these pools. I miss fishing in the Pacific Ocean, seeing the brown pelicans diving and the seagulls. I miss my family!"

"I do too," replied Six-Pack, "but I'm really nervous about this drone. What if something goes wrong?"

"Everything is going to be fine," Alice replied. She patted his head with her flipper."

Anyway, it is worth the risk, just to get home!" She swam another circle around the pool.

Sergio and Sabrina have a discussion with their mother,
Maryann Sulla, on the deck of their Sausalito home.

CHAPTER SIX

Family Struggles with Deadly Pandemic

Maryann Sulla sat on the deck of her Sausalito home with a cup of coffee and the morning newspaper. She took a minute to gaze at the yacht harbor below. She was a trim woman who exercised regularly at home and hiked when she could. Her hair, a light brown color, was cut short. It was quite a contrast to her two children who inherited her Italian-American husband's black wavy hair and dark skin tones.

Maryann's eyes were bluish-green while the children's were brown, in fact Sabrina's were almost black and always seemed to sparkle when she was excited.

Maryann was tired this morning. She worked as a flight attendant and had just returned from the long round-trip flight to Kona, Hawaiii. Maybe it was time to retire, she thought. But she had always loved flying and being able to see places she had only dreamed of visiting as a young girl growing up.

There had been those years when Sergio and Sabrina were still toddlers when she had stayed home to be with them. But then after the children started school the offer came for her to return to work at the airline, and she accepted it. Sabrina and Sergio's grandmother lived nearby, which was a lifesaver now that the schools were closed and the children had to study online.

Maryann thought about her job. Now, with COVID-19, it wasn't much fun anymore. Flights were being cancelled all the time, and when they did go, the planes were only a third full. And while the passengers were carefully cleared at the airports for any signs of sickness, there was always the chance that a "carrier" who showed no signs of illness might slip through and board a plane.

Only residents of Hawaii seemed to be flying these days—just to get back home. Suddenly her days of travel and excitement at seeing the world had been transformed into. . .into what? The world was definitely a much more complicated place now.

Sergio and Sabrina bounced out to the deck, but they looked more serious that usual. Maryann wondered what was going on.

"Where's Dad?" Sergio asked.

"He left for the hospital about an hour ago for an early staff meeting," Maryann replied giving each child a hug. "What's up?"

"Oh, we were just wondering what you thought about the pandemic," Sabrina said, dishing herself up some scrambled eggs and toast that her mom had left in the oven for them.

"It's awful!" her mom replied. She gave an involuntary shudder.

"But how long do you think it might go on?" Sergio asked joining them with his own plate of food to which he had added some fresh blueberries.

"I really couldn't say," Maryann replied. She got up to fill her cup with coffee. "What Daddy has said is that we need a well-tested vaccine that absolutely works. Then that needs to be produced, and then a nation-wide vaccination program must be put in place.

Sabrina and Sergio looked at each other knowingly. Maryann saw the look of understanding pass between them and tried to think of what it could mean. "We will just have to take it one day at a time," she said. "Continue with your school online and social distancing of six feet, and wear a mask—and don't forget to wash your hands. I know how hard it is for you children to be cooped up like this, not able to see your friends. At least you have each other."

• • •

The Marine Mammal Council met again that night and Alice, the harbor seal, reported on her progress getting the humans to help them.

"Yes," she said. "Sergio and Sabrina Sulla appear to be quite sympathetic to our plight and our desire to return home so we can warn our families to stay away from humans!"

Sergio studies photographs and sketches of military
drones on a computer in his bedroom.

CHAPTER SEVEN

Sergio Searches for Military Drones

Sergio finished his online school assignments, then began to search for any information on drones. He had once flown a small drone at Stinson Beach. It was owned by a photographer friend from Sausalito and was just big enough to carry a camera. The drone was used mainly for taking photos from the air, shots of big outdoor events or houses being put on the market for sale or rent. It was also just plain fun to take a picture of a group of people having a picnic on the beach or sunbathing.

Who would have thought of using a big drone to transport marine mammals back to their homes? Actually Sergio decided it was a fabulous idea and really might work.

Sergio continued to read and found that drones were used during World War II as targets. Fighters and anti-aircraft gunners needed something to shoot at that would not endanger humans.

The name came from bees, the ones that are heavier than worker bees. In the Fall they leave their hive and swarm. They seem to have a mindless existence and don't gather honey or defend their hives but can be heard buzzing around the female.

In the last few years the term, "drone," has become more common. Sergio found a section online that advertised drones with cameras for sale. Some cost hundreds of dollars and other thousands. There were even some listed that cost less than $100.

Sergio then searched online for military drones, and that was an entirely different thing. They were called "UAVs," which stood for "Unmanned Aerial Vehicles." Photographs showed some very slick models with pointed noses and small wings and tails. One had a long pole sticking out of its nose. Another was called "Silver Bullet."

Sergio read on. "The Sky Hawk," the information said, "operates virtually automatically. The user merely hits the button for 'Take Off' and or 'Land' while the UAV drone gets directions by satellite and reports back with a live feed."

There were some fancy names for the military drones such as "Global Hawk," "Tritons," "Reapers," and "Shadows." They were mostly designated for surveillance or carrying cargo or missiles. Sometimes they were referred to as "RPA's" or "Remotely Piloted Aircraft."

Sabrina came into Sergio's bedroom just as he was about to turn off his computer. "Did you find anything about drones?" she asked.

"Yes, you want to read it all?" Sergio asked. He was quite excited about the drone at The Marine Mammal Center and looked at his little sister with new respect.

"I sure would!" she replied. She had noted a shift for the better in Sergio's attitude toward her and was pleased.

"OK. I'll forward it to you," he said and emailed all the information to her. Then he turned off his computer and scratched his head. He wondered if there might be information attached to the drone itself. He would need to get down into the old missile silo where the drone was stored to see what the machine looked like. But how could he to do that?

It was hours later and Sergio had already gone to bed. He was nearly asleep when he heard a ping. He raised up on an elbow and looked at his cellphone on the night stand. He had a message from his friend, Nicky, a guy on his high school swim team. It said, "If you get this, call me. Nick."

Sergio sat up to look at his watch. It was nearly 11:00 pm. He turned on the light by his bed and rubbed his eyes. What could his friend want at this hour? Picking up the phone he found Nick in his contact information and hit the call sign.

His friend answered immediately in a whisper, "Hello."

"What's up?" Sergio whispered back.

"I don't know if this is true," Nicky said, "but you know one of my little sisters is a friend of your sister, Sabrina."

"Yes," Sergio whispered hoping no member of his family could hear him talking.

"Well, Nicky continued, "Sabrina told my sister about a drone she claims is at The Marine Mammal Center. I just couldn't believe it. She said it was a big one, too, used by the Navy or Coast Guard. Is that true?"

"Hmmmm," Sergio said stalling for time. So much for their secret. Well, it was going to get out soon anyway.

"Is it true?" Nicky repeated, his voice a little louder.

"Yes," Sergio replied. "It was brought here by a Coast Guard Commander."

"What for?" Nicky asked.

"The people at the Center are thinking of using it to return the harbor seals, otters and sea lions to their original homes. With COVID keeping the Center closed, many of the animals can't get home. The Center doesn't have all the volunteers they had before to get the animals back to their original colonies."

"You mean you could fly them home in that thing?" Nicky asked.

"They are thinking about it," Sergio replied. "Boy, I'd sure like to ride in one of those machines!"

"That could be really dangerous," Nicky said, his voice much louder. "When my sister told me about this I spent some time online looking up military drones. There have been some serious accidents using them!"

"Oh, I guess," Sergio replied. "I know you are right. But you could get hit by a vehicle in a cross walk or drown swimming in the ocean with all the rip tides."

"You're right," Nicky conceded. "Did I ever tell you about my Uncle Fred who got killed on Thanksgiving Day walking across the street?"

"Sorry to hear that," Sergio replied yawning," but I want to go to sleep now. I'll call you when I know more about it."

The boys clicked off their phones, and Sergio tried to go back to sleep. As he lay in the dark he thought about what it would feel like to ride in a big drone with somebody else far away in control of the unmanned plane.

Did You Know?

Did you know that sea lions have external ear flaps and seals don't?

Sergio and Sabrina pull back a tarp covering a military
drone named the "Neptune" stored in an old silo at
The Marine Mammal Center, a former NIKE site.
They are caught by Commander Bud Nicholas of the
United States Coast Guard.

CHAPTER EIGHT

Kids Caught Taking Photos of Hidden Drone

Alice, the harbor seal, solved the problem the next time Sergio and Sabrina stopped by the Center. "Caroline stores a lot of our food down in the silo," Alice said popping up from her pool. "She goes down there two or three times a week. The drone is down there, too."

Sergio nodded and walked up to the kitchen where Caroline was blending fish shakes for the remaining marine mammals. As usual the young woman appeared to be smiling, but that was hidden because she was wearing a mask.

"Hey, Caroline," Sergio called out. "Can I go down into the silo with you one day? I'm helping Sabrina write a report on military coastal defenses built around the Bay Area. Actually she would like to go also to see where the NIKE missiles were stored and maybe take some pictures."

"Sure," Caroline replied. "I've got a whole bunch of stuff that needs to be taken down and stored, and you kids could help carry. How about in an hour?"

"Sounds good," Sergio replied and went to find his sister.

An hour later, Caroline, Sergio, and Sabrina headed for the silo. They helped push carts loaded with supplies. Watching Caroline closely, Sergio discovered that the lock on the silo had the same combination as the lock at the entrance of the facility. One never knew when that knowledge might come in handy, Sergio thought. A huge door opened, and they stepped onto a gigantic elevator floor.

"The missiles used to be raised and lowered on this elevator," Caroline explained. The area was very dim and sort of looked like a huge cave. When they reached the bottom, Sergio and Sabrina helped Caroline store boxes of frozen fish in the big freezers.

"Can we look around?" Sergio asked.

"Take your time," Caroline replied. "I think I'll go back up for another load if you don't mind being alone down here for a few minutes. It's kind of spooky!"

"We're fine," Sabrina said and watched as Caroline climbed on the massive elevator and went back top side.

"Over here," Sergio called to Sabrina. "Toward the back on the right side."

Sabrina hurried over just in time to see Sergio pull up the corner of a canvas covering something. Both kids gasped to see the shiny silver drone revealed under the tarp. It had large helicopter blades and what looked like long inflated pontoon skis, plus small wheels.

It was just as Alice had described. A small manual of information was tucked into a pocket of the tarp. and Sergio pulled it out. The manual was titled, "NEPTUNE XXL10,—TOP SECRET." Sergio slipped the manual into his pocket just as he heard the elevator start back down.

Sergio was taking pictures with his cell phone when the door opened, and a tall, gray-haired man in a uniform strode out of the elevator.

His eyes were blazing. "WHAT ARE YOU KIDS DOING DOWN HERE?" he snarled. "GET AWAY FROM THAT DRONE!"

"We came down with Caroline," Sabrina said. Then working up her courage she asked, "Who are you?"

"Commander Bud Nicholas of the United States Coast Guard," the man barked. "I got this drone for the Center and I don't want anyone messing with it! Put that tarp back where it belongs!"

"Sure," Sergio said. "I was just taking a couple of pictures. I think it is important that it be used as soon as possible."

"Oh you do, do you?" the Commander asked. Behind his mask he had a craggy, weather beaten face and frowned as he continued. "You kids are aware that a pandemic is going on?"

"Of course," Sergio replied noticing that the Commander was wearing a mask. "But I believe that it is important that this project to return the healthy marine mammals to their homes should continue, and this drone would really speed things up."

As the Commander began to understand their plan, a slow smile crinkled his eyes, and he seemed to relax his ramrod military posture. "Well, you've got guts, I'll say that! Who are you kids?" he asked walking over in the dim light to inspect them closer.

Sabrina answered, "I am Sabrina Sulla, and this is my brother, Sergio. We live just down the hill in Sausalito. We have been coming up here for years. Sergio wants to study marine science, and we both want to volunteer here when we are old enough."

"Well, I guess you weren't doing any harm, and we both have the same goal," the Commander said with a small hidden smile.

They all heard the elevator going up and then back down. The door opened, and Caroline appeared carrying more supplies.

"Oh hi, Commander Nicholas," I see you have met Sabrina and Sergio."

"Yes," he replied. "Caroline, isn't it? I'm just checking on my Neptune drone. Fine young people, Sergio and Sabrina. They want to get this project moving too."

"We all do," Caroline replied. "Good to see you, Sir." She turned to put the food supplies away.

Did You Know?

Female elephant seals can dive to almost 6,000 ft. (1,800 metres). And while the average dive time is 23 minutes, the longest recorded by a female elephant seal was almost two hours.

Sergio and Sabrina, back in Sergio's room, read
over the manual of the Top Secret Neptune.

CHAPTER NINE

Sergio and Sabrina Study Neptune Drone XXL10

Back home in Sausalito Sergio and Sabrina poured over the manual on the Top-Secret Neptune drone stored in the silo of The Marine Mammal Center.

"It says," Sergio reported, "that the Neptune should be run by a UAV (Unmanned Aerial Vehicle) operator who works for a contractor who pilots and maintains UAVs. This drone is protected from lightning and has reinforcements to the air frame."

Sergio continued, "The Neptune can remain aloft more than 30 hours and go as high as 35,000 feet with speeds up to 300 MPH. It has a multi-function active sensor (MFAS) X-band AESA radar with a 360 degree field of regard."

"I think that means the on-board sensors can scan all the way around." Sabrina sat and listened totally fascinated. "WOW!" was all she could think to say. She wasn't sure what all that meant but it sounded important.

Sergio continued. "Operators only need to choose an operating area for the Neptune and set an altitude, direction and speed. This drone is built with more robust lower fuselage to withstand bird strikes and weather such as hail and lightning."

Sergio pulled out his cell phone and looked at the pictures he had taken of the Neptune drone.

Sergio and Sabrina show Maryann photos Sergio
took on his cell phone of the drone.

CHAPTER TEN

Plans Are Made to Push Drone Idea

It was a sunny morning in Sausalito and Maryann had decided to risk going out on the deck with her coffee and the *Marin Morning Standard*, her daily newspaper. She hoped it wouldn't be too windy.

She was only half way through the paper when Sabrina and Sergio joined her. "Shouldn't you be going over to Grandma's for your online classes?" she asked.

"It's Saturday," Sergio replied with a chuckle.

"Oh, right!" she exclaimed. "I've been flying so much I just lost track."

"I want to show you some photographs," said Sergio pulling out his cell phone.

Maryann looked with interest at the photographs of the Neptune drone. She also felt a bit of apprehension, wondering what was going on.

"What in the world is it?" she asked.

Sabrina's dark eyes sparkled with excitement as she quickly jumped into the conversation. "It's a Neptune Drone XXL10 that is stored in the old NIKE silo at The Marine Mammal Center."

"For what reason?" Maryann asked setting down her newspaper. Now she was really confused.

"A military guy whom we met at the Center, named Commander Nicholas, who is in the U.S. Coast Guard, wants to acquire the drone and donate it to The Marine Mammal Center. It has to be tested first, though" Sabrina continued.

"Why would the Center want it?" the mother asked.

This time Sergio answered. "For the release of the marine mammals when they are all healthy again. Instead of trucking the animals to the beach and then having to lug heavy carriers down to the shoreline, this drone lifts up like a helicopter. It can land on water, and is remotely operated through a satellite system. When it lands, a door opens and the marine mammal drops out and swims away."

"That sounds like a great idea. Where did you get the photos?"

"We went down into the silo yesterday," Sergio said and handed his mother the booklet about the Neptune. "That is where we met the Commander Nicholas."

"Where did you. . ."

Sergio interrupted her to explain. "It was tucked into a pocket in the cover of the Neptune. I will return it."

Maryann studied the manual. "This says 'TOP SECRET!'"

Sergio continued to explain. "I know. It's a military drone that didn't pass some inspection. I think the defect has been corrected but it has to be tested before it can be sold."

Maryann asked, "How much will it cost and who is going to pay for it?"

Sergio shook his head. "I have no idea of the cost but probably a lot! I don't know who will pay for it. Maybe it's being donated."

"But how are you involved?" asked Maryann, concerned.

Sergio and Sabrina looked at each other and hesitated. They had agreed not to mention their friend Alice, the talking harbor seal.

"Well," Sabrina said, "the animal releases have slowed to almost nothing since all the volunteers have been let go. And they need volunteers to either carry the animal carriers or wheel them down to the water, and everyone has to take a separate vehicle to get to whatever beach has been scheduled."

"Mom, did you know," Sabrina continued, "that this is the middle of the pupping season when the Center has a lot of patients? So if the Neptune could be tested and if it works safely, it would free up space to help more sick animals."

Maryann stared hard at her children. Sometimes the things they came up with absolutely amazed her. Still, she felt she might not be getting the whole story.

"If you are really concerned," she said, "why don't both of you go talk to Michael London, the CEO of the Center. I met him last year at a fundraiser, and he seemed like a really nice man, someone who would listen. Call The Center and make an appointment.

"Well, it's Saturday," Sabrina observed, "but let's try, Sergio."

Her big brother looked up the phone number on his cell phone and punched in the numbers.

"The Marine Mammal Center," a woman answered.

"Hi! This is Sergio Sulla. I would like to make an appointment to meet with Michael London."

"Sorry," the lady replied. "Dr. London is out of the state for at least two weeks."

"Ask about a Board of Directors meeting," Maryann suggested. "You could talk to them directly."

"Could I make an appointment to speak at your next Board of Directors meeting?" Sergio asked.

"I'm sorry," the lady replied, "that is impossible also. Because of the pandemic, everything is cancelled until further notice."

"O.K., well thank you," Sergio said politely and clicked off his phone.

The three of them sat there silently for a few minutes.

Finally Maryann suggested, "You might want to go to the media, even the social media. An article in our local newspaper might stir up some interest and get this moving. Let me see if I know any of the editors." She thumbed through her morning paper looking for the information.

"Wait!" cried Sabrina. "I have a girlfriend at school whose father is an editor, I think. Is there someone named Mr. Lawrence?"

Maryann looked at the masthead carefully. "Yes! There is a Matt Lawrence. He's the City Editor. Maybe he could assign one of his writers to cover a story on the Neptune drone."

"My friend is Karlie, Sabrina said. "I will call her right now."

David Duckster, a reporter and photographer for the
local newspaper, interviews Sergio and Sabrina.

CHAPTER ELEVEN

Kids Are Featured in Drone News Stories

It all worked out. Sabrina called Karlie Lawrence who spoke to her father who said that he wanted to see Sergio's pictures. After examining them, he assigned a reporter to follow up.

David Duckster, a reporter from the newspaper and wearing a mask, came to the house in Sausalito to interview the children out on the deck while keeping a six-foot distance.

The reporter, a man in his forties who was beginning to show a little extra weight around the waist, was very friendly asking a lot of questions and shooting a few photographs of Sergio and Sabrina. He said he would let them know when the article would appear, but he had several more calls to make. Duckster was impressed with the kids and they formed a fast friendship. Maryann felt very pleased that she had suggested this course of action.

A week later Sergio received a text to let him know that the story would be printed in the *Marin Morning Standard* the next day, which would be on Monday. And so it appeared on the front page of the local news section with pictures of Sergio and Sabrina.

SAUSALITO STUDENTS PUSH FOR DRONE TESTS

By David Duckster

Sausalito, CA – Sergio Sulla, age 13, who is a student at Tamalpais Middle School, and his younger sister, Sabrina, age 9, who attends Wake Grammar School, are pushing for tests to be conducted on a Neptune XXL10 Unmanned Aerial Vehicle. Better known as a drone, the Neptune was built by the U.S. military for use by Navy Seals.

This highly classified piece of equipment is temporarily stored in the old NIKE site at The Marine Mammal Center in Sausalito. It is on loan for possible use as a way to release fully recovered marine mammals cared for by the Center. Toxic illness, entanglement with fishing nets, or even being shot could have brought them to The Marine Mammal Center, their only hope for survival.

The Neptune UAV was obtained by Commander Bud Nicholas of the United States Coast Guard. He helped develop the UAV program, which began in the Navy and was later picked up by the Coast Guard. He lives in San Francisco and has long been a supporter of The Marine Mammal Center.

Commander Nicholas first began working with the unmanned aircraft system (or drones) executed by the Naval Air System. It marked a rare occasion for the U.S. Navy and the U.S. Coast Guard to work together developing a new program.

In a short phone interview, the Commander explained that this particular drone was rejected by the Navy because of problems with its surveillance capabilities.

He was able to obtain it for a try-out in the animal release program at the Center because it can rise straight up like a helicopter and land on water. A halt to the testing came when everything shut down because of the coronavirus pandemic.

The news article brought an amazing response from the public. Phone calls, letters-to-the-editor, Tweets and other social media flooded the *Marin Morning Standard* offices.

Maryann, Sergio, Sabrina, and even their father, Dr. John Sulla, read the paper eagerly every morning. In a follow-up piece by David Duckster, Sergio was quoted as saying, "In normal times I would have my friends out with big signs picketing at the Center to move ahead with the drone testing, but big groups aren't allowed these days."

Commander Nicholas added to his original statement that the Navy was threatening to take the Neptune back if it wasn't going to be used. "How about a test flight between Sausalito and San Francisco near Pier 39," he suggested. "If all goes well, we can begin with the release of the sea lions, especially Hugo who was shot in the chest. I understand that he is completely recovered now."

This caused The Marine Mammal Center Board of Directors to hold an emergency ZOOM meeting, since they were unable to meet in person. The members, sitting in front of their own devices listened attentively as Commander Nicholas addressed them. He explained how he would arrange for a test with a drone programmer to set the destination, altitude, and speed needed to fly the drone to San Francisco and then back to Sausalito.

The test was approved by the Center's Board of Directors and by the military. A date was set for Saturday, May 2, and the local population as well as members of the Center would be able to watch by webcams set up at The Marine Mammal Center and at Pier 39 in San Francisco. All Bay Area airports and the Coast Guard were notified of the test flight.

Sergio and Sabrina show Alice, the harbor seal,
the newspaper article with their photograph.

CHAPTER TWELVE

Operation "Drone Home"

Sergio and Sabrina bicycled back up to The Marine Mammal Center to talk to Alice. "I thought this was supposed to be a secret," the roly-poly harbor seal complained waving both her front flippers at Sergio. "Now all these people are involved. If they aren't flying the drone, they're watching someone else fly it. I thought this was just our project," Alice cried. "What is going on?"

"Look Alice, maybe I'm the best video gamer of my friends, but there is no way I know how to handle a drone this complicated," Sergio replied. "I read there are drone operators who are specially trained for this job. It would be risky for me to try to operate the drone. The pros have to take over from here."

Alice dove into her pool and swam a couple of laps. Dripping wet, she hauled herself back up on the side.

"And," Sergio continued, "don't worry, we won't say that we got the whole idea from a talking harbor seal!"

Sabrina spoke up. "I brought the newspaper if you want me to read you the article about the Neptune." She was clearly very excited.

Alice muttered, "Hhhmmm. Well, I've heard most of it but go ahead."

Sabrina quickly read through David Duckster's article, which was followed by a few Letters to the Editor.

"The Letters to the Editor show that there's a lot of interest in all this," Sabrina said holding up the newspaper. "Listen to this letter. The writer is a boy who says he is 14 years old, and guess what—he goes to school with Sergio.

Dear Editor, I really want to take a ride on the drone. I have been saving up my allowance and could pay for a ticket if this is possible. Please call or text me at the number below.

Sabrina didn't bother to read his phone number. "Here is another," she continued, "from a girl. I know her. She is in my English class."

Dear Editor: Is it really true about the drone? Can we see it somewhere? Signed Samantha Louis, age 10, Wake Grammar School.

"So," Alice said, "it looks like people are excited about what we want to do. I guess they plan to test the drone next Saturday, right?"

"Yes, we are supposed to be able to watch on a webcam, but we will be able to see Neptune lift off right here from this pool area," Sergio said.

Alice shot up from the bottom of her pool shaking water all over Sergio. "We can call this "OPERATION DRONE HOME!" she cried excitedly.

Did You Know?

Did you know that northern elephant seals eat fish and squid and sharks and rays?

Commander Bud Nicholas meets with Jack
Marfield at Marfield's office in Mill Valley.

Commander Hires Drone Operator

Commander Bud Nicholas, who had gotten the Neptune drone for The Marine Mammal Center, met his friend, Jack Marfield, at Jack's office in Mill Valley. Jack was a retired UAV (drone) programmer for the United States Navy.

"How do you like retirement?" Commander Nicholas asked Jack. The Coast Guard Commander was a tall man, 6-foot, 3-inches, who used to be a baseball player. He had mousy brown hair, brown eyes, and a heavy jaw. This day he was wearing a military uniform with lots of ribbons and medals. There wasn't an ounce of fat on him anywhere.

Jack was a little shorter, 5-foot, 10-inches, and he also was slender. He laughed. "Retired? I've never been so busy since I retired from the Navy and opened my own 'Drone Operator' business—that is until COVID-19. By the way, that is quite the fruit salad you're wearing on your chest!"

The Commander smiled. "Well, I have a meeting with some military brass later this afternoon, so I had to wear the uniform. Anyway, that's great, Jack, about your new operation," the Commander continued. "Who are your clients?" He pulled up a chair and sat his lanky frame down. Jack rested on the edge of his desk.

"Anyone who owns a drone and needs an operator," Jack explained. "I do surveying and mapping, take real estate photos, serve the media, and law enforcement. I hunt for someone who's lost or even a missing airplane. I shoot entertainment photos, even spray for agriculture or mosquitoes. Shall I go on?"

Commandeer Nicholas laughed. "OK, I've got the picture. It has always seemed to me that operating a drone is a lot like playing a video game. You serve as an external pilot and directly control the flight by sight. That must include the launch, mission, and recovery or landing."

Jack lowered his mask and smiled. "You should know. You got me into that program, and it's pretty unusual for a Coast Guard Commander and a Navy guy to be working together. I thank you for that. Now, what is the mission? "

Commander Nicholas explained about The Marine Mammal Center, the Neptune drone, and returning the animals to their homes.

"How old is the Neptune?" Jack asked.

"Roughly six years old," Commander Nicholas replied. "I don't think it is classified anymore. The Army, Navy, Air Force and Marine Corps all have their own drone programs now. Have you heard about the Navy Flimmer?"

"I think so. Is that the one that flies, lands on water, dives and swims?" Jack asked.

"That's it! It is much smaller than the Neptune but has amazing capabilities!"

Then the Commander asked, "Are you familiar with the operation of the Neptune?"

"Sure," said Jack. "That one should be easy." He moved around to sit in the chair behind his desk.

The two men began to discuss the landing of the drone in San Francisco Bay to return the sea lions to Pier 39.

"As you know, "Commander Nicholas said, "there are Bottlenose Dolphins, porpoises, gray whales and humpback whales in the bay right now. I think the last count was eight gray whales.

"The whales are migrating from their breeding grounds in Mexico," the Commander continued "to their summer feeding grounds in Alaska. They travel 10,000 miles during migration. It is very tough, and they are hungry. Some have been coming into San Francisco Bay looking for food. They gulp or lunge for anchovies and other fish. The whales get entangled with nets or long crab pot lines, or sometimes they are hit by ships. Many of the huge container ships are larger than sky scrapers."

Jack pulled down a map and spread it out on his desk. "I see there are two sanctuary zones, The Monterey

Bay National Marine Sanctuary and beyond that is the Greater Farallones National Marine Sanctuary."

He pointed to a spot on the map near the city. "We could possibly land the Neptune in the 'Exclusion Zone,' if they'll give us permission."

"Why is that there?" Commander Nicholas asked.

"The area was designated an 'Exclusion Zone' in the 1980s to make a place where big ships can operate" Jack replied. "The Exclusion Zone was designed to act as a sanctuary. In the 'Sanctuary Zones' big ships are required to slow down during migration so the whales aren't struck. The problem is many ships don't obey those rules."

The Commander thought about it. "I know the Coast Guard is in charge of all vessel traffic so you will have to work with us. When we land to release the sea lions, I will make sure a Coast Guard cutter is out there to see that all the marine mammals are out of the way."

"How many sea lions are there to go?" asked Jack as he folded up the map.

Commander Nicholas thought for a minute. "It will take three trips. The first to test the safety of the drone, then two more each carrying two sea lions without carriers."

"Maybe," he continued, "I will also arrange for a diver to be sure that when the door opens the sea lions swim out. On some releases the animals don't want to leave. But I think they will hear the barking of the hundreds of other sea lions that have hauled out at Pier 39, and they will want to join them."

"Sounds like a plan," said Jack, "so let's get working on the details."

When the big day arrived to test the Neptune, Sergio and Sabrina bicycled up to the Center to watch the action.

Did You Know?

Did you know the Northern fur seal mothers carry their babies 12 months before they are born?

The drone, filled with sea lions being
taken to San Francisco, lifts up into the air
at The Marine Mammal Center..

CHAPTER FOURTEEN

Sea Lions Fly to San Francisco Bay

Usually there would be a big crowd to observe such an important event, but people were forbidden to gather because of COVID-19. They went immediately to see Alice. The fat little harbor seal was swimming excitedly around her pool. She was happy to see her human friends.

"We had a celebration last night," she reported, "with lots of whooping and splashing and barking! We are all so happy about Operation Drone Home. I especially wanted to say 'Goodbye' to Hugo, Humphrey, Lisa, and Lynn, sea lions who will be going back to their families on Pier 39 in San Francisco."

"Do you know what time the Neptune is scheduled to take off for the test?" Sabrina asked looking at her watch.

"Mid-morning is all I've heard, after the fog lifts." the harbor seal replied.

"Let's go up to see the missile silo." Sergio said to Sabrina.

The two of them left the pool area and were just arriving at the entrance of the NIKE silo when they heard the big doors open. A couple of minutes later they both gasped as the Neptune XXL10 was raised up on the missile elevator.

Just then they saw the newspaper reporter, David Duckster, arrive, carrying a camera. He saw them and called out, "Hey Sergio! Sabrina! Come on over here. I want a photo of you both in front of the Neptune. You kids really got things moving! Congratulations!"

Sergio and Sabrina ran over and stood in front of the drone with faces blushing as Duckster took several photographs.

"Thanks for your articles!" Sergio said, "especially your research and tracking down Commander Nicholas. Do you think he will be here today?"

"Yes," Duckster replied. "He's right over there."

"Commander! Bud!" Duckster called. "I want you to meet Sergio and Sabrina Sulla who got this project going."

The tall military man came over to say "Hello" but did not shake anyone's hands because that was forbidden under COVID-19 rules. "I have already met Sergio and Sabrina. Great going!" He said. "You both should be very proud!" Under their masks, everyone was, grinning and although Sabrina wanted to give the Commander a hug, she knew she shouldn't.

Sergio and Sabrina thanked him again and scampered back to their viewing place. They stared at the Neptune.

It was a shiny silver color and seemed to be larger than when they had seen it before half hidden under a tarp.

They both noticed the small wheels attached outside the pontoon landing skis. The wheels made it possible for the men who were assigned this job to move the drone quite easily.

"We'd better get out of the way" Sabrina whispered.

"Right," Sergio replied. Sergio saw Caroline come out of the kitchen to watch, too.

The Neptune was carefully moved into a clearing in front of the elevator that had once been used for storing the missiles.

The kids waited for what seemed like an eternity as the men moved around the drone, adjusting certain features, and monitoring weather conditions.

Finally all the technicians backed away and the blades on top started rotating slowly, then faster and faster and louder and louder. Sabrina covered her ears. Her heart was pounding as she and Sergio were battered by the wind and noise the drone produced. The drone lifted slowly up into the sky and then headed south toward San Francisco. They watched intently as it flew away, disappearing over the hills.

"Wow!" Sabrina exclaimed. "That was awesome! Isn't there a webcam set up at Pier 39 so we can see the landing in the bay?"

"I think so. Let's ask Caroline," Sergio replied. He and Sabrina adjusted their masks to cover their nose and mouth.

They hurried over to the kitchen and found Caroline sitting in front of a large computer. Still wearing her mask, she waved them over. "Somebody set up three of these monitors throughout the Center so the staff that is still here could watch the landing."

The children pushed forward eagerly to get a look at San Francisco Bay on the monitor. The only vessel in view was a Coast Guard cutter. Then suddenly there it was, the Neptune Drone coming in for a landing on San Francisco Bay.

Caroline, Sergio, Sabrina, and a few members of the staff found themselves jumping up and down, shouting and bumping elbows. It looked like a perfect landing.

Then the camera zoomed in on a door opening into the Neptune. "That must be where the sea lions will come out," Sergio said.

Next they saw some men climb into a small skiff from the Coast Guard ship, which motored over to examine the drone. Everything must have looked okay, because the crew soon returned to their ship.

Suddenly the Neptune was rising up out of the water and heading north, back to The Marine Mammal Center. It was soon out of sight on the computer monitor but within minutes they heard what sounded like a helicopter as the drone reappeared in the sky above them. A few minutes later it landed back in front of the NIKE silo.

Sergio and Sabrina felt the wind from the drone's whirling blades and watched some men in front of the Neptune talking on cell phones.

Then one of the men yelled, "Test operation complete. Everything A-OK! Bring up the sea lions, two at a time!"

Sabrina gasped as she saw Hugo and another sea lion being wheeled in carriers up to the NIKE site loading area. Hugo passed their viewing place and seemed to have spotted them. He raised a flipper and waved "Goodbye!"

"Do you think he is fitted with sensors or a radio or something so his handlers will know he made it back to Pier 39?" Sabrina asked her brother.

"Oh sure," he replied. "I'm not certain what they use these days but they always attach some device to track the release. I don't think it stays on forever, but for a while anyway."

Sergio and Sabrina watched breathlessly as the live sea lions disappeared into the Neptune.

It only took another fifteen minutes before the drone was airborne again and headed for San Francisco Bay. When it was up in the air and out of sight, Sergio and Sabrina joined Caroline in the kitchen to watch the photos being taken by the webcam that had been set up to see the Neptune land.

Suddenly there it was coming down out of the sky to land on its big ski-shaped pontoons. S P L A S H ! ! ! The drone skidded to a stop, rocked up and down a few times, then settled down on the water.

As before, the camera zeroed in on the door of the Neptune, and a diver appeared. Then, suddenly the door opened—but nothing happened. Everyone held their breath, waiting for the sea lions to appear. The diver swam over and looked inside. Still nothing happened.

Then the diver swam back and forth, and, finally, a head appeared in the opening.

"It's Hugo!" Sergio cried.

Hugo looked around cautiously. . .and around. . .and around. Then, after about ten minutes, he waddled out followed by Herbert, or maybe it was Lisa.

Once in the water the two sea lions swam quickly out of sight heading toward Pier 39 and the sound of hundreds of barking sea lions.

"We've got to go tell Alice that they made it," Sabrina said to Sergio, and the two of them raced to the harbor seal's pool.

It wasn't long before the Neptune returned to The Center and the other two sea lions were loaded up and flown out.

They also arrived with no problems and exited much faster than Hugo had. So the operation was a brilliant success.

Now it was time to plan for the release of the harbor seals, otters, fur seals, and Toby, the young elephant seal.

To the kid's surprise, the Sunday morning paper printed on the front page the photograph of them standing on their deck at home and on the back page another photo of The Marine Mammal Center.

Did You Know?

Did you know that seals have smaller flippers than sea lions?

Sergio and Sabrina read about the Neptune and
see their photo on the front page of the *Marin
Morning Standard.*

CHAPTER FIFTEEN

Kids' Photos Appear in Sunday Newspaper

"You are getting to be famous!" their mother teased.

"Aw Mom," Sergio protested. "Do you think the article got all the facts straight?"

"Looks all right to me," Maryann said and passed the newspaper to the eager kids to read for themselves.

"It says, " Sabrina noted, "that more releases will be done this week, but the newspaper is not allowed to announce the schedule because too many people might try to watch when they should be sheltering at home."

Sabrina gave a deep sigh. "Oh I wish this pandemic would hurry up and end. When are things going back to normal? My hands are getting cracked from washing them so much, and this mask is a real pain!"

Her mother nodded. "Everyone feels the same way, but no one actually knows when it will end. We just have to wait it out."

The Neptune lands in the water at Pier 39 in San
Francisco where many sea lions are swimming
frantically around disturbed by the noise of the drone.

CHAPTER SIXTEEN

Plans for More Seal Releases

It was late Monday morning when Commander Bud Nicholas returned to the office of Jack Marfield, the UAV programmer who had operated the Neptune drone.

"Great job! Congratulations on a perfect mission!" exclaimed Commander Nicholas to Jack. He was clearly happy.

"Thanks!" Jack replied. "Did the sea lions make it back to Pier 39?"

"You bet!" the Commander said. "And it only took them twenty minutes. You know they can swim twenty-five miles per hour. Amazing! Here is a photo of the landing."

Jack studied the photograph and smiled. "Incredible job!" he exclaimed. "But we need to plan the rest of the releases as soon as possible. There is some talk that businesses will be able to open back up soon. Right now it is no problem to donate my time to this operation since everyone else is shut down."

"I have a list of the marine mammals and where they should be released," Commander Nicholas said laying a folder down on Jack's desk.

"The three Pacific harbor seals should be released in the Bolinas Lagoon. That is the place, next to Stinson Beach, where they haul out and breed.

"The sea otters will just have to be flown down the coast to Monterey where they live in kelp beds," Commander Nicholas continued."

"What about the northern fur seals?" Jack asked.

"There are several places we could choose. First is San Miguel Island off of Santa Barbara on the southern coast of California. Closer to San Francisco," the Coast Guard Commander continued, "is the recently re-established rookery of fur seals on the Farallon Islands. They are a pretty short hop west of here, only twenty-five miles. Before a release spot is chosen, we will have to find out where the fur seals were rescued."

"What about the young elephant seal?" Jack asked. "I know there are large breeding grounds on the Point Reyes Peninsula near the Point Reyes Lighthouse. I think it is called Chimney Rock."

Commander Nicholas thought about it. "It's pretty rough in the Pacific Ocean out by the Lighthouse, but we could land in Tomales Bay just off Lawson's Landing. Or if it is a real calm day, Drake's Bay would be good, too. Anyway, let's get this mission underway!"

If we land in Drakes Bay, how are we going to get the elephant seal to Chimney Rock, near the Point Reyes Lighthouse?" Jack asked.

"Good question," Commander Nicholas replied. "Maybe we will just have to truck the elephant seal out to West Marin. He is probably too large for the drone anyway. Looks like we have to take this one day at a time."

Did You Know?

Did you know that female elephant seals can dive to almost 6,000 ft. (1,800 metres)?

The Neptune flies over the Golden Gate Bridge.

CHAPTER SEVENTEEN

Neptune Flies Marine Mammals Home

The next week was busy and exciting as all the releases were coordinated and carried out. Sergio and Sabrina bicycled up and down the hills between The Marine Mammal Center and their home to watch flights of the Neptune.

On the day of the next drone release, Sergio and Sabrina cycled up to Conzelman Road, one of the roads leading to Fort Cronkhite. From there they would have a spectacular view of the Golden Gate Bridge and San Francisco Bay. They wanted to see the Neptune fly over the bridge. They arrived just in time to watch the silver drone passing over the orange-red bridge, a magnificent sight.

David Duckster wrote up reports on all of the releases so everyone could keep up. Sometimes he mentioned that Sergio and Sabrina Sulla of Sausalito had been the driving force for the whole operation. The kids were slightly embarrassed but secretly enjoyed it. And since there was no school, their friends could not tease them except by phone or text.

Sergio, sleeping in his bed, dreams about
flying in the drone..

CHAPTER EIGHTEEN

Sergio Plots a Dangerous Flight

Sergio lay on his bed staring at the ceiling and replaying in his mind the release of the sea lions in San Francisco Bay. How exciting that had been. He was certain that he wanted to study and spend his life in marine science.

To think that he could actually communicate with Alice, the harbor seal, amazed him. What would it be like when she returned to the Bolinas Lagoon and saw her family again? Could all of them talk? Or maybe some?

Sergio sat up in bed and turned on a small light. He reached for a glass of water and swallowed nearly half of it in one gulp. He knew all the rules of the pandemic were getting to him. He hadn't been able to see his friends, play high school baseball, or participate in swim meets.

He had always been an outstanding swimmer. Now all the pools were closed, though his swim team was training in San Francisco Bay.

He hadn't complained or whined about it. His sister had to give up her tennis just when she was really getting good at that sport.

Sergio turned the light back off and stretched out, his thoughts returning to the Neptune drone. The seed of a crazy idea was beginning to form in his mind. The Neptune had been built to transport Navy Seal divers, so there must be oxygen and some kind of light inside. He could check that out along with its weight capacity.

Maybe—just maybe he could squeeze inside the Neptune and go with Alice, the harbor seal, back to the Bolinas Lagoon when all the harbor seals were released.

When the Neptune landed in the Bolinas Lagoon, he could swim over to Kent Island to watch the celebration when Alice and the other harbor seal, whose name he couldn't remember—Six-Pack, maybe that was it—met up with their family and friends.

Then after he dried off a bit, he could catch a bus in Stinson Beach, which was within easy walking distance, for a ride back to Sausalito. He wouldn't be doing any harm. No one would even need to know what he had done.

Sergio struggled to get to sleep. What would it be like to ride—to actually fly in the drone?

He sat up and turned the light back on. Then he thought for a while about going down to the kitchen for another piece of the chocolate cake that his mother had surprised them all with, except he wasn't really hungry.

His thoughts returned to the drone. Maybe, just maybe he would do it! He could wear his wet suit hidden under his clothes—just in case he needed it. No one would notice except maybe his sister. Sabrina seemed to see everything.

He finally turned off the light and lay in bed thinking of how it would feel to fly in the Neptune with two harbor seals. It was another hour before he finally fell asleep.

Alice and Six-pack, two harbor seals, are loaded
into the Neptune. Sergio is hiding inside.

CHAPTER NINETEEN

Sergio Stows Away

Sergio and Sabrina with COVID-19 masks in place, were standing in front of Alice's pool saying, "Goodbye."

"My Mom and Dad promise to drive us out to see you one of these days," Sabrina said.

"You two be safe and thanks for arranging all this," Alice said. "We marine mammals will make sure to tell the story. Now we know that there are smart, caring humans!"

The youngsters stood back when a couple of volunteers showed up with a carrier to take Alice, and then Six-Pack, up to the Neptune.

It was another exciting morning. Today would be the last releases of this amazing week when all the marine mammals would be going home.

Sergio and Sabrina walked behind the carrier not talking, when suddenly Sabrina said to her brother, "Is that your wet suit you are wearing under your clothes? Why are you wearing that?"

"Shhhhhhh!" Sergio responded.

Then Sabrina noticed that Sergio was also wearing a waist pack. "What are you up to?" she asked feeling worried. The look on her face was one of intense concern. They were almost at the launching site, and the Neptune was in view.

They had reached their favorite viewing spot and slipped temporarily out of sight. Sergio pulled off the long heavy boots they always had to wear when walking around the pools.

Please return these for me," he said. "I'm going for a ride to the Bolinas Lagoon with Alice! Don't tell anyone!"

"You can't do that!" Sabrina cried. "What if something goes wrong? You could be killed!"

"Shhhhhh!" he admonished her. "It will only take about half an hour to get there. I'll walk over to Stinson and catch a bus home."

"That's crazy!" Sabrina cried and started to go outside looking for someone to stop her brother. She turned back to confront him again, but he was gone. She looked everywhere but knew in her heart that she would not find him, because Sergio had found a way to sneak into the Neptune and accompany Alice and Six-Pack, two now healthy harbor seals, to their home in the Bolinas Lagoon.

Did You Know?

Did you know that all the northern elephant seals we see today—170,000— are living on the Pacific coast?

As the drone approaches the beach, the door falls open
dumping the two harbor seals into the Pacific Ocean.
Sergio falls after them.

CHAPTER TWENTY

Seals and Sergio Are Pitched into the Ocean

Sabrina's heart was pounding wildly as she watched the Neptune lift off the pad and head west toward the Pacific Ocean. Then, the silver drone turned north to follow the coastline up to Stinson Beach and the Bolinas Lagoon.

Like all the other Neptune trips, this one had been cleared with the Coast Guard and all the local airports. But no one except Sabrina knew that a human being, her own brother, Sergio, was inside this time.

When the Neptune was out of sight, Sabrina ran up to the kitchen where she knew Caroline would have a webcam connection set up to watch the Neptune arrive at the lagoon.

Inside the Neptune, Sergio was drinking from his water bottle. The two harbor seals were lying on the floor watching him intently. Sergio actually had a bench to sit on, one of two he figured were built for the Navy Seals. There was even a tiny peephole he could look out. After all the week's releases, the inside of the drone smelled really fishy, but there was fresh air coming in from two vents, so they could all breathe fine.

"Does anyone know you are with us?" Alice asked. She stared hard at Sergio, as the light was pretty dim. They also were experiencing some heavy vibrations and loud noise from the drone engines and the blades on top. Six-Pack tried to be brave, and Alice attempted to comfort him.

"Not exactly," Sergio replied. "I did tell Sabrina." He leaned over to peer out the peephole and could see a few clouds and the Pacific Ocean below.

"I'm so happy to be going home!" Alice said. "Have you ever been to Kent or Pickleweed Islands in the Bolinas Lagoon?" she asked.

Sergio thought back. "Yes, once I took a canoe over to the islands from the harbor in Bolinas. There were several of us in canoes, and we paddled all around the lagoon." He had to shout over the noise of the Neptune.

"That's where I got my name," Alice said, "from Kent Island which is named for Alice Kent." Six-Pack, the other harbor seal squirmed around but remained quiet.

"Wow!" Sergio exclaimed. "Who was Alice Kent?"

"She was from the Big Island of Hawaii, and she married Roger Kent. His parents supported conservation causes. The town of Kentfield is named after the Kent family. Sergio was listening with rapt attention. He had friends who lived in Kentfield.

Suddenly they seemed to be descending quite sharply. Sergio looked out his peephole but could only see the blue Pacific Ocean coming closer and closer.

Then there was a loud CRACKING sound. The door of the Neptune flew open. With terrified eyes, Sergio saw Alice and Six-Pack slide right out the door and disappear. He could barely hear their bellowing barks over the noise of the Neptune's engines, which had increased when the door opened. Sergio grabbed hold of the bench he was sitting on, but the Neptune began to pitch downward toward the ocean. He could barely hang on.

The Neptune increased its fall, and that made holding on to the bench impossble. Losing his grip, Sergio felt himself sliding toward the open door. "Oh no, no, no! he yelled as he slipped uncontrollably out of the Neptune. As he fell toward the water, he automatically straightened himself into a diving position. When he hit the water, he sliced it clean going down. . .and down. . .holding his breath and feeling cold and dizzy and lost. Could he find the way back up? Good thing he wore his wet suit. He hoped it would give him enough buoyancy to reach the surface.

Sergio began to kick frantically, using his arms like paddles as he tried to reach the light above him. Finally, in what seemed like an eternity, he broke the surface of the water gasping and choking on several mouthfuls of seawater.

But where was he? Which way was land? He knew that great white sharks lived in these waters, and his treading water could attract them. Could he reach a beach? Which way should he go? All he could see was the ocean all around.

It was nearly noon, and the sun was directly overhead, so that was no help in figuring out his directions. If he swam the wrong way, he could be lost at sea. He was still cold and disoriented.

He treaded water turning around and around trying to see land. And then he saw a familiar face. It was Alice, the harbor seal.

She swam right up to him. "Can you swim?" she asked.

"Yes," he replied coughing still more water from the ocean. "But I don't know where to go."

"Follow me," me said. "If you get too tired you can hang on to me too. I will take you to the entrance of the Bolinas Lagoon. It is at the end of a sand spit called Seadrift. The town of Bolinas is on the other side."

"THANKS!" Sergio shouted spitting out more seawater.

Alice swam slowly enough for Sergio to follow, and within fifteen minutes they had reached the sand spit where Alice left Sergio on the beach.

"There is a road that will take you right into Stinson Beach," Alice said.

"You saved my life! I don't know how I can ever make it up to you!"

"Thank you for bringing us here," Alice replied. "Sorry you will miss my family reunion. At least none of us was seriously injured. Try and come out and see me sometime. I'm usually on Pickleweed Island, near Highway One." Waving a flipper, Alice swam off while Sergio lay on the warm sand, glad to be on shore.

Sabrina and others watching a monitor
at The Marine Mammal Center, see two
harbor seals and her brother, Sergio, fall
from the drone into the ocean.

Sabrina Sees Sergio Fall

Back at The Marine Mammal Center, Sabrina had been watching on Caroline's computer the drama caused by the defective door of the Neptune.

Everything had been going well when the Neptune began drifting down and then suddenly, while still in the air, it's door opened and the two harbor seals came tumbling out.

Then Sabrina screamed when she saw her brother slide out behind them. She was stricken with terror when she saw Sergio plunge into the vastness of the Pacific Ocean. The drone flew on to the Bolinas Lagoon and landed safely, but the door was still open, and it began to take on water as it bobbed up and down on its pontoons. Sergio was nowhere in sight.

A group waiting for the landing paddled over in a small boat and peered inside the Neptune. It was empty.

The group in the boat looked out at the ocean in disbelief. What had happened to the harbor seals? One of the men pulled out his cell phone to call the Coast Guard.

"We have an emergency here," he shouted into the phone. "The drone arrived but the door was open and it was empty! The two harbor seals are lost somewhere out in the ocean!"

The Coast Guard officer on duty replied, "Oh, I think they can find their way home. They are in the ocean every day feeding aren't they?"

"Yes, but never so far out!"

"They'll show up. Give me a call when they arrive."

Twenty minutes later the men talked again. The harbor seals had made it to Pickleweed Island, looking really weary.

Meanwhile the men had heard about the missing stowaway. In fact the whole Bay Area watching the drone on computer monitors and television sets had seen the stowaway falling from the Neptune into the Pacific Ocean. Emergency calls were being made to anyone who could possibly help.

Another boat showed up at the Neptune. Men with buckets climbed into the half submerged drone and began bailing out water that had poured in from the Bolinas Lagoon.

It would take several hours to remove all the water, get the drone back in an upright position and begin drying it out with battery charged fans. Dozens of towels were used to dry the inside while the fans were still whirling.

TV crews arrived from San Francisco to cover the clean up operation. But the big question throughout the entire Bay Area was about the stowaway. Who was he, why was he in the drone, and had he drowned?

Did You Know?

Did you know that:

- Harbor seal have spots and are smaller and lighter than other seals?
- Sea lions have big chests and tiny ears and are larger animals?
- Seals have ears only on the inside with just small holes on the outside where ears would be?

Alice, the harbor seal, swims up to Sergio
and guides him to the shore.

CHAPTER TWENTY-TWO

Sergio's Survival

When Sergio made it to shore, he collapsed, exhausted on the Seadrift Beach and fell asleep. Some loud noise woke him up a bit later. He stared into the cloudless sky and saw helicopters buzzing overhead. Out on the ocean Coast Guard patrol boats were motoring back and forth. He thought that it must have been the noise of the helicopters that woke him up. He felt very weak and did not know if he could walk. He knew that he had almost drowned and could still taste the seawater in his mouth. He discovered he was barefoot. He had unconsciously kicked off his shoes to making swimming easier.

He still had his pack around his waist, and he unbuckled it. Thankfully, his bottle of water was intact, and he gratefully gulped some down.

Next he dug out his cell phone, which he had put in a tight, water proof bag because he had thought he might have to swim in the lagoon. He opened the bag and found the cell phone dry, but the glass was smashed. The phone was absolutely destroyed.

Sergio looked around the beach and saw several groups of people sunbathing. He staggered over to a group of teenage girls stretched out on beach towels.

"Does anyone have a cell phone I could borrow?" he asked. "Mine just got smashed," he added showing them his cell phone. "I need to make a call."

The girls looked at this strange boy in ripped, soaked clothes with a wet suit underneath. He looked kind of sick. Who was he?

They had been having a nice peaceful afternoon and within the past hour everything had gotten very noisy Motor boats, airplanes, even helicopters were suddenly everywhere.

Now this guy had appeared out of nowhere. He looked a mess, like he had been swimming in his torn clothes, and he seemed to have left his shoes somewhere. He had nothing on his feet, not even flip-flops.

"Who are you?" one of the girls asked, "where are you from and how did you get here?"

"Where is your mask?" the other girl inquired.

"It's a long story," Sergio said, "and right now I really, really need to make a phone call. Can I use your phone?"

The two girls answered at the same time. "Sure!" Both held out their phone, and Sergio gratefully took one.

It looked just like his cell phone, an iPhone. He studied it for a minute as he decided whom he should call and then punched in a number.

Did You Know?

Harbor seals come out of the water almost daily to rest and to warm up. They cannot maintain their body temperature if they stay in cold water all the time because of their smaller size and thinner blubber layer.

Sergio borrows a cell phone from some girls
sunbathing on the beach and calls his sister.

CHAPTER TWENTY-THREE

A Desperate Call to Sabrina

Sergio punched in his sister's phone number. She answered immediately. She was crying.

"Hey!" he said. "It's me."

"OH MY GOD!," Sabrina cried. "YOU'RE ALIVE! HE'S ALIVE," she screamed to the crowd around her. "Where are you?"

"I'm at the north end of the Seadrift Beach at Stinson."

One of the girls chimed in: "Tell them you are near the tennis courts."

"Near the tennis courts," Sergio added. "Do you think Mom could come get me? I don't think I have the strength to walk down to town."

"Everyone is searching for you!" Sabrina told him. "The Coast Guard has helicopters and boats out. There is even an ambulance at the park to take you to the hospital in case you were found alive. The Stinson Beach Fire Chief has been patrolling up and down the sand. Whose phone are you using? I didn't recognize the number. How can Mom reach you? She's pretty hysterical."

"My phone got smashed," Sergio replied, "so I borrowed one from some girls here on the beach."

"Are they going to be there for a while?" Sabrina asked.

Sergio asked the girls, and they nodded yes. "Our parents are renting a house out here for a month, so we're not in any hurry to get back over the hill," one girl said. Then she added, "We used to come out here for just two weeks but the COVID-19 rules say to rent a house out here now requires a 30-day minimum stay. I like that!"

"Yes." Sergio nodded to the girl and said to his sister, "Mom can call me at this number."

"Boy, what a splash you made!" Sabrina told him. "Thousands of people were watching that final release of the Neptune and saw both harbor seals and then you fall into the ocean."

"Did Alice and Six-Pack make it back?"

"Yes," Sabrina said. "You know they always attach tracking devices on the marine mammals that are released. Both Alice and Six-Pack showed up on Pickleweed Island in the Bolinas Lagoon just as they were expected to."

"How am I going to get home? And how soon?" Sergio asked. He was feeling dizzy again and sat down on the sand.

"The Fire Chief is on his way. He will take you to the ambulance, which will take you to the hospital to check you out," Sabrina told him.

"Tell them I'm sorry, Sabrina. I didn't mean to cause all this fuss."

"It's OK! Everyone here is so happy to know you are alive. I've got to call Mom now. See you at the hospital."

Within a few minutes the cell phone rang and it was Maryann and John, Sergio's parents. He told them what had happened. Then he handed the phone back to the girl who had loaned it to him. The girls were looking at him in wide-eyed wonder.

"Are you the one they are searching for? Is that why the boats and helicopters are all buzzing around?" one girl asked.

"Yes," Sergio replied.

"Here," another girl said. "You can lie here in the shade of this umbrella, and we will watch for the rescue people."

Sergio thanked her, lay down on a towel under the umbrella, and passed out

Another article appears in *The Marin Morning Standard* about a "Teenage Stowaway" in the drone..

CHAPTER TWENTY-FOUR

Near Disaster for the Drone

David Duckster wrote the story for the *Marin Morning Standard,* which was picked up by most of the nationwide newspaper syndications and social media outlets.

NEAR DISASTER FOR NEPTUNE DRONE AND TEENAGE STOWAWAY

By David Duckster

Sausalito, CA – Thousands of people were watching on their computers, iPads, and cell phones when the Navy's Neptune XXL10 drone, had a near disaster today. As Neptune began its descent to the Bolinas Lagoon, the door of the main hatch unexpectedly flew open while the drone was 25 feet above the choppy ocean surface below.

Suddenly, the Neptune pitched violently downward, tossing two harbor seals and one human stowaway into the sea. They fell from roughly the same height as a two-story house.

Around the world, people watching the drone mission on webcams, shared the shock of witnessing the accident. How could this have happened? What was a teenage boy doing in

(continued on next page)

a drone? Did he survive the trauma of being dumped into the Pacific Ocean?

It turns out that the live human was thirteen-year-old Sergio Sulla of Sausalito. This is the same young man who, along with his younger sister, Sabrina, have been the driving force behind using drones for the release of marine mammals.

Thankfully, Sergio Sulla survived the fall and was able to swim to the beach at Seadrift, Stinson Beach, where he was picked up by the local Fire Chief Michael Branden and transported by ambulance to the hospital. He is said to be recovering.

So why did he stow away in the drone? Sergio claims he is fascinated by marine mammals and wanted to be at the site when the harbor seals returned to the Bolinas Lagoon. He wants to study marine sciences and work in that field when he grows up.

Because of his young age, the Marin District Attorney's Office has declined to press charges, but he will have a hearing in Juvenile Court on June 15.

He has apologized to everyone for the distress he has caused. He admits that his little adventure was a stupid thing to do and promises never to attempt anything like that again.

Accompanying the article were two photographs of Sergio and Sabrina taken at The Marine Mammal Center. One was in front of the Neptune, and the other by the harbor seals pool.

A follow-up article appeared on June 16 after Sergio's appearance in Juvenile Court. The judge, a woman, was unusually lenient in Sergio's case, because no one was seriously injured, and there was no real property damage. In addition, the judge was a supporter of The Marine Mammal

Center, and she admired everything else that Sergio and Sabrina had done to help the stranded seals find a way back home. She sentenced Sergio to doing fifty hours of community service, cleaning up the local beaches and hiking trails, and four weeks of home probation.

The judge, Samantha Shore, charged Sergio with a misdemeanor which she explained was a minor wrong doing.

By this time Sergio had been appointed a Public Defender named Tracy Beachum who appealed to the District Attorney to lower the fifty hours of community service to twenty-five hours. "Sergio Sulla is showing a strong sense of responsibility to the community," Public Defender Beachhum said.

The Public Defender also requested the fine of $500 be cut in half to $250 and home probation lowered from four to two weeks.

After some discussion, the District Attorney, Jeannette Jordan, agreed to request the judge make these changes Judge Shore said she would take it under advisement.

It was three weeks before Sergio and his family heard back that Judge Shore had agreed to lower the penalties.

During this time Sergio also found a way to return the Neptune manual to its home in The Center, just in case it might be needed again

Alice, the harbor seal, is reunited with her
family on a tiny island in the Bolinas Lagoon.

CHAPTER TWENTY-FIVE

Alice Reunites with Her Family

One day Commander Bud Nicholas was unexpectedly contacted by the United States Department of the Navy. They informed him that they wanted the drone, Neptune XXL10 returned to them immediately. Among some other matters, the Navy needed to figure out why the door had malfunctioned and then to have it repaired. There was also a secret assignment for some Navy Seals that had to be executed right away.

Commander Nicholas informed The Center, and with Jack Marfield's help, they flew the Neptune back to the naval base in San Diego, California.

Fortunately, most of the marine mammals had all been released. Sergio had returned home from the hospital after two days of observation. He was weak but growing stronger and had developed an appreciation for using better judgement before making risky assumptions. Sergio would have plenty of time to think this over during his probation period, which was scheduled to start immediately. His clean-up duties were planned for July and August.

One night during dinner at the Sulla house, Dr. Sulla announced that he was exhausted from his work at the hospital because of all the COVID-19 patients. Then he straightened up and smiled.

"When the pandemic is under control, probably when a vaccination is available, I think all four of us should go over to Kona, Hawaii for a week or two. We can visit Ke Kai Ola, the satellite hospital that The Marine Mammal Center built to try to save the endangered Hawaiian monk seals. There's so much to do on the whole island. I'm sure you kids would like to see Volcano National Park, spend a few days on the beach, and maybe even attend a luau. How does that sound? And we wouldn't have to worry about getting the virus." He looked at his wife and children encouragingly.

He saw smiles slowly appear on the kids' faces.

"Promise?" Sabrina asked.

"PROMISE!" their dad replied raising up his hand. "We all need something to look forward to."

The Sulla family looked forward eagerly to the end of the pandemic and to their vacation on the Big Island of Hawaii. They would celebrate the end of the COVID-19 threat. Little did they know that the situation would get a whole lot worse before it got better.

That evening Sergio and Sabrina sat talking about their upcoming adventure in Hawaii, and then they wondered how Alice was doing at home in the Bolinas Lagoon.

And back at the lagoon, Alice, happily reunited with her family, thought about her daring drone ride and the scary release back to the ocean. Alice hoped to see her new human friends again, someday soon! Who else would know she could speak English?

www.ingramcontent.com/pod-product-compliance
Lightning Source LLC
Chambersburg PA
CBHW061539050726
47593CB00002B/835